I0829503

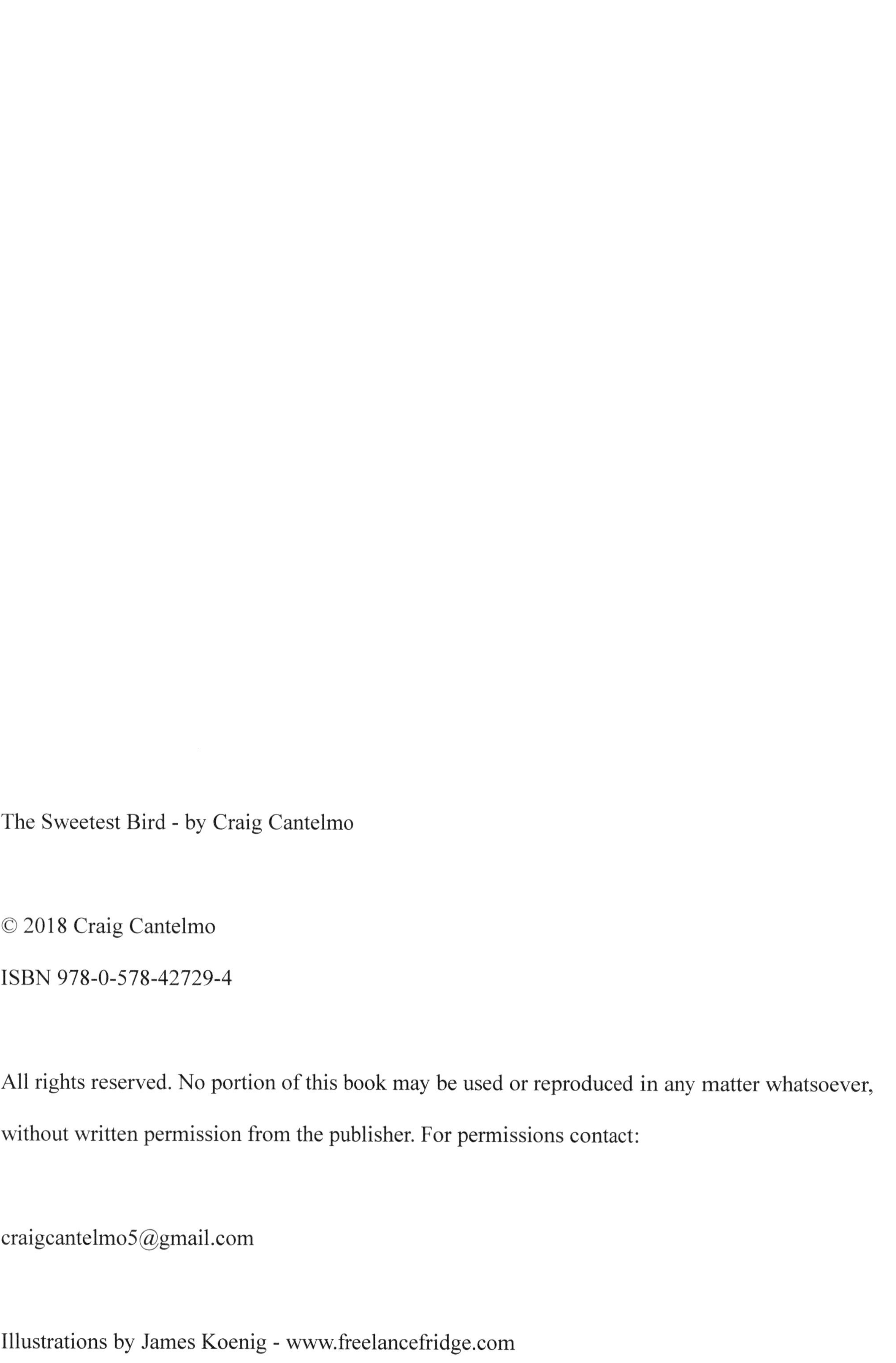

The Sweetest Bird - by Craig Cantelmo

ISBN 978-0-578-42729-4

Illustrations by James Koenig - www.freelancefridge.com

To Aiden and James

- Mr.C -

To my future children,
may the stork find his way to us soon

– James Koenig –

The Stork is a bird
And I give you my word,
His voice is the sweetest
That I've ever heard.

His two favorite colors
Are pink and light blue.
This is for good reason,
Believe me it's true.

I will try to explain,
Don't mind if I do.
The pink is for girls
And for boys, baby blue.

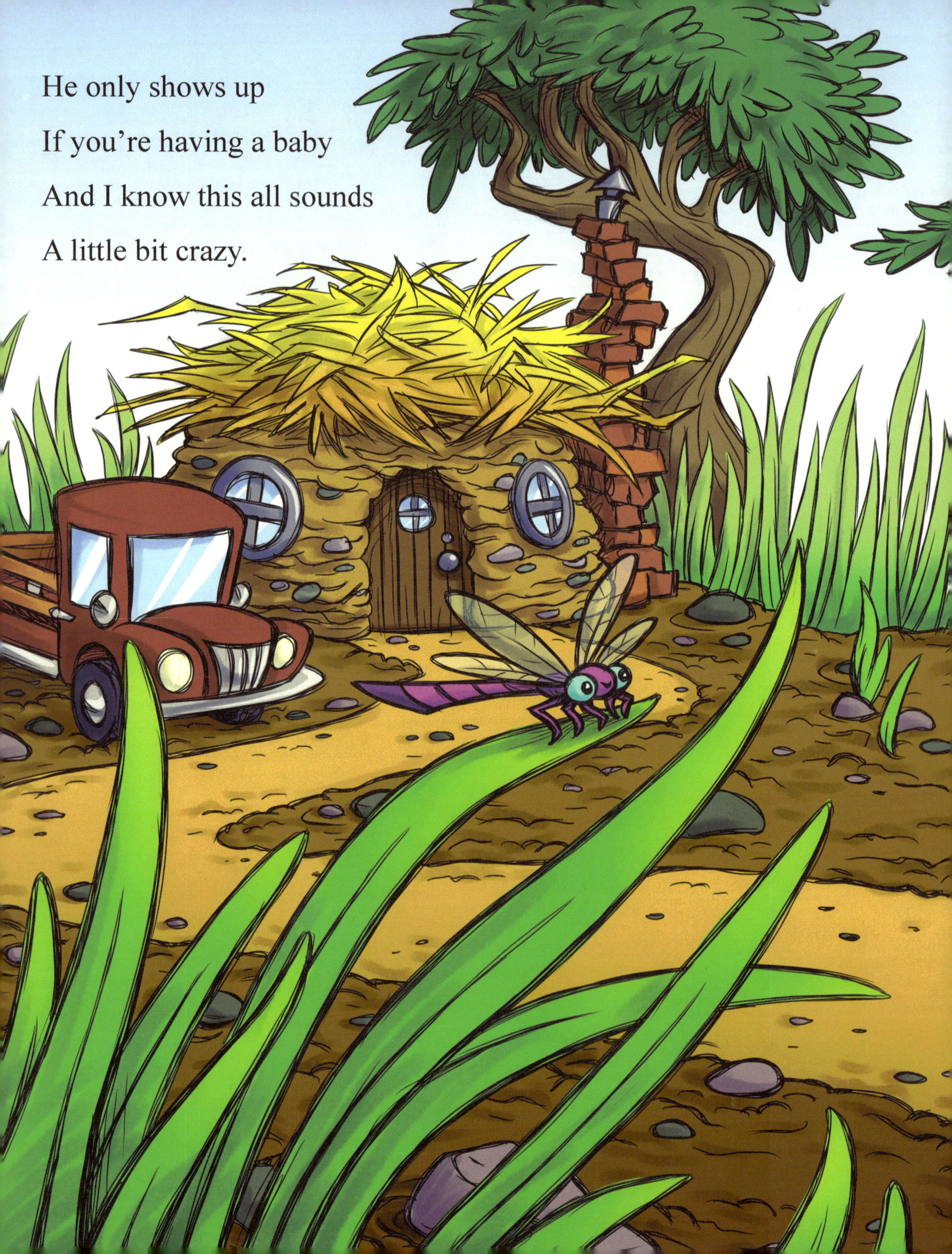

He only shows up
If you're having a baby
And I know this all sounds
A little bit crazy.

But if you are blessed,

He is probably coming.

And he is usually singing,

Or dancing, or humming.

Sometimes he calls

To tell you he's coming,

And sometimes my friend,

It's late that he's running.

Sometimes this guy
Will show up unannounced.

And sometimes he's so late

That you start to lose count.

But when he does come,
He comes with a smile.
He shows up with love
And he might stay a while.

HANDLE
WITH
CARE

Some babies are bald

And some come with hair.

Regardless, he tells you

To, "Handle With Care."

Sometimes your babies
They look just like you.
And sometimes some things
Might be under review.

The eyes of some babies
Are a beautiful blue
And your uncle will say,
"Hey, my eyes are blue too."

The leaves come and go
But your babies will stay.
They will crawl, walk, and talk
And then want to play.

He dresses amazing.
Believe me, I swear.
Then he stands nice and tall,
And he brushes his hair.

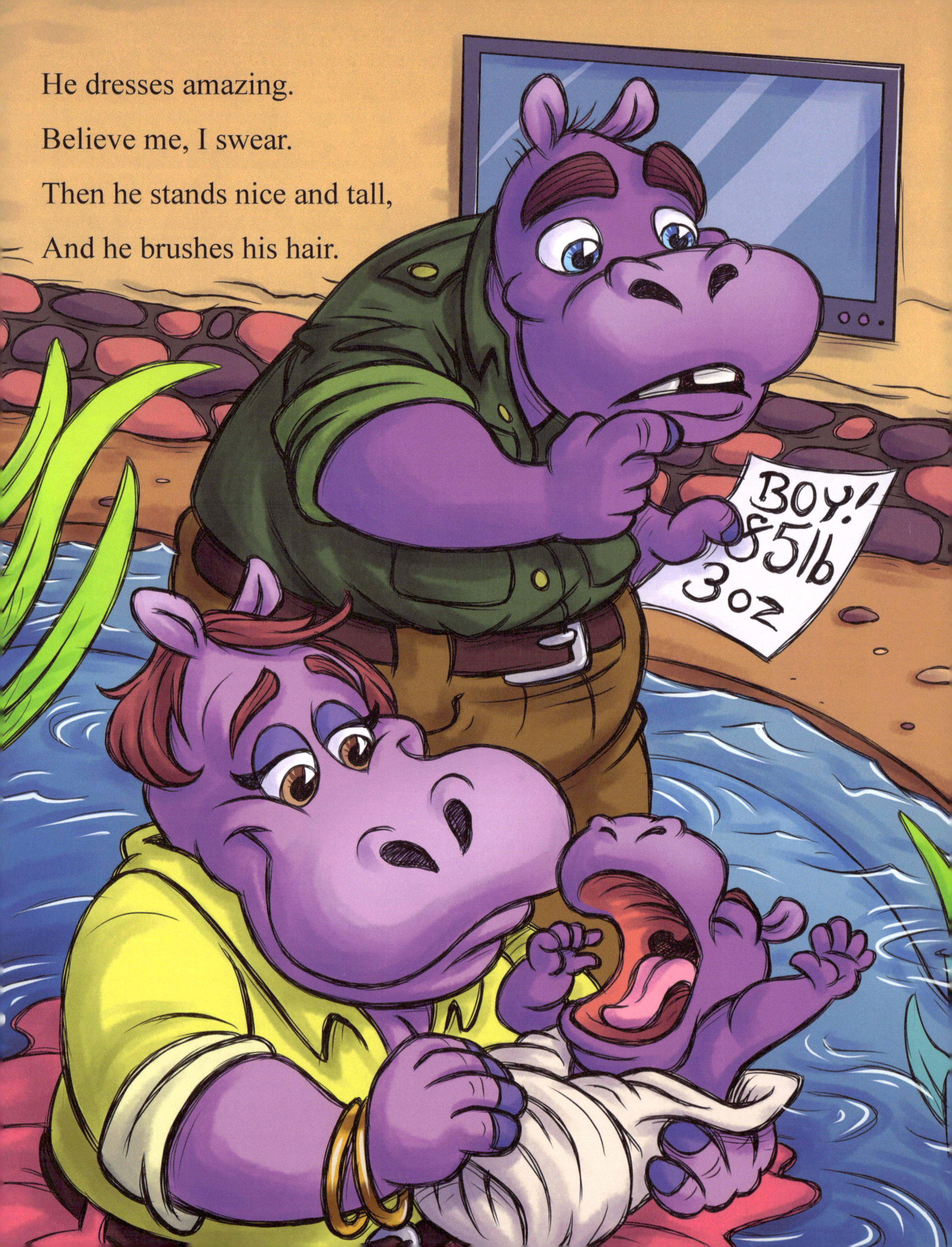

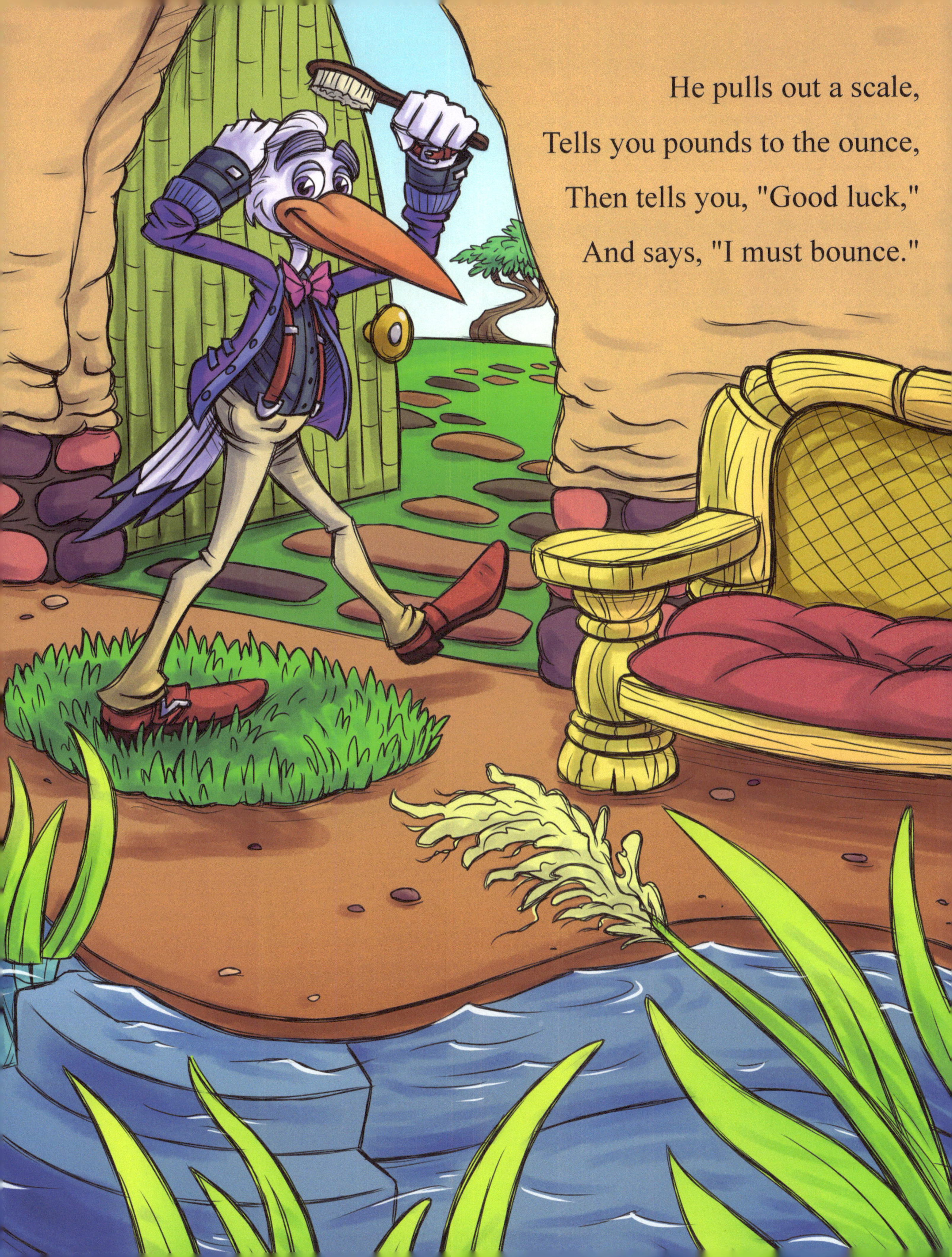
He pulls out a scale,
Tells you pounds to the ounce,
Then tells you, "Good luck,"
And says, "I must bounce."

And his words, his words
His voice and his words.
They are the sweetest in all
Of the kingdom of birds.

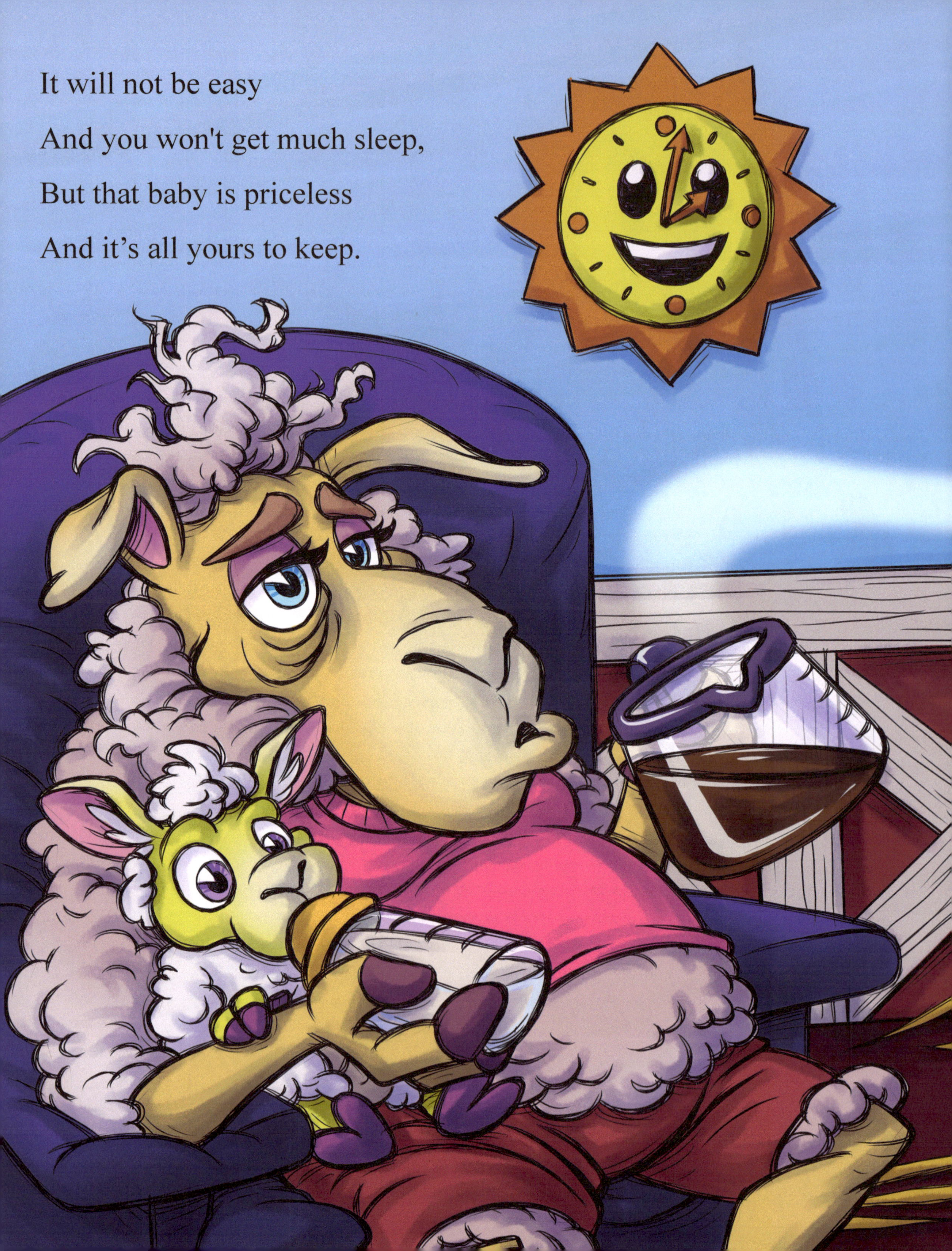

It will not be easy

And you won't get much sleep,

But that baby is priceless

And it's all yours to keep.

Cute as a button
And soft as a sheep.
Boy, oh boy,
The benefits you reap.

He leaves no instructions,
Or directions with sections,
Or scientific formulas
With mathematic connections.

$$\frac{365(\heartsuit !)}{Q_3 + 100\%^5}\left(\frac{\sum(z^6)}{A_1 e + \oint}\right)$$

(ABC) + $ + ☺
E=MC²
123 +
A
C B
√
π +
H₂O +
cos(X^YZ - 55^-13)
HAPPY BABY!
=

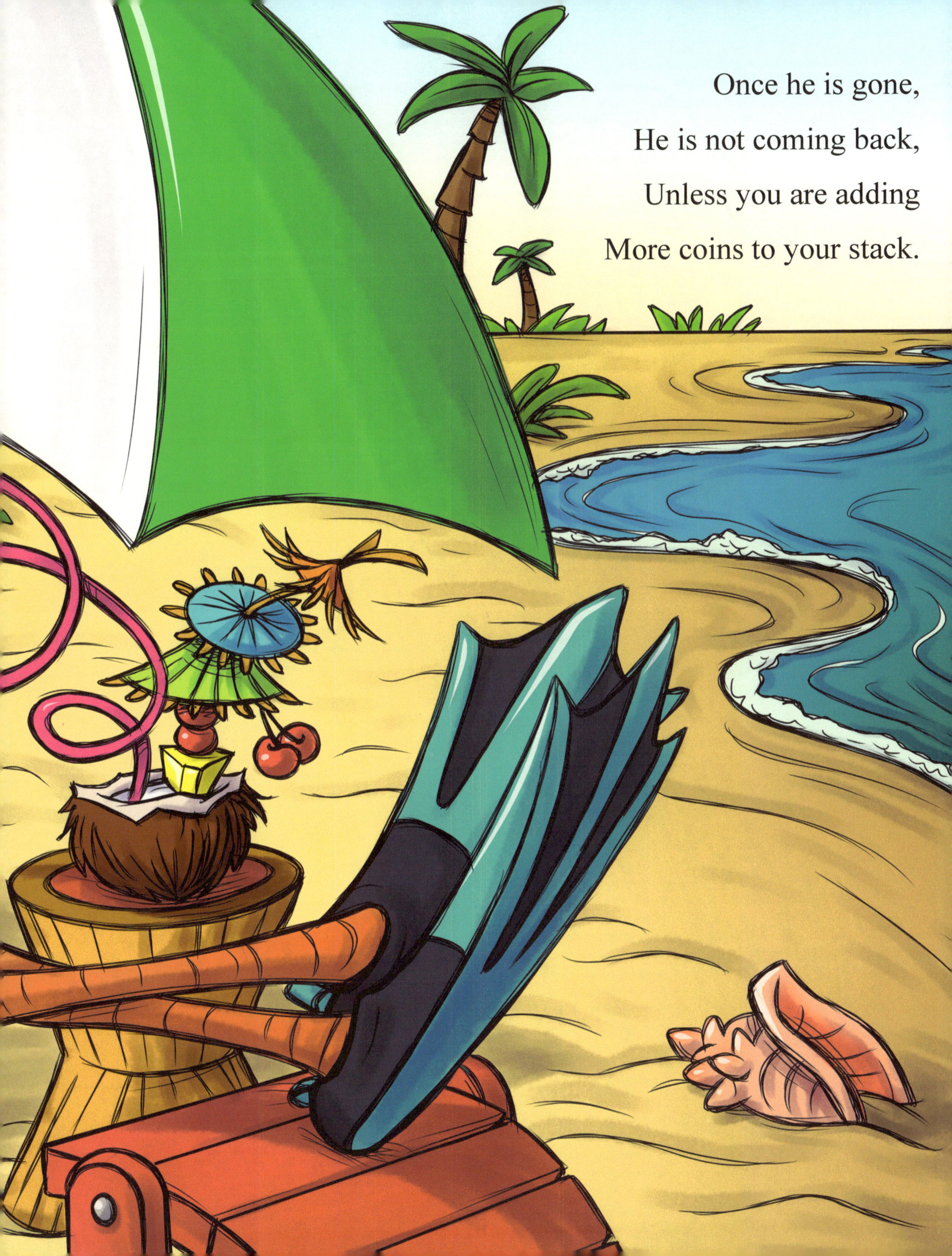

Once he is gone,
He is not coming back,
Unless you are adding
More coins to your stack.

But if you are adding,
Then yes he is coming.
And I bet that he looks
Incredibly stunning.

He's remarkably smooth
And awfully smart.
I believe this is how
Your journey will start.